For my four-legged
You were always there.

And for Jack, Eloise, Elias, and Wendell —
My inspiration.

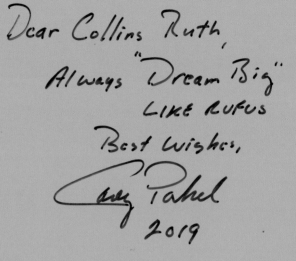

Dear Collins Ruth,
Always "Dream Big"
LIKE RUFUS
Best Wishes,
Carey Pahel
2019

www.mascotbooks.com

Rufus the Mild-Mannered Bull: Rufus Saves the Day

For more information, please contact:
Mascot Books
620 Herndon Parkway #320
Herndon, VA 20170
info@mascotbooks.com

Library of Congress Control Number: 2018905694

CPSIA Code: PRT1118A
ISBN-13: 978-1-64307-033-9

Printed in the United States

RuFus the Mild-Mannered Bull

RuFus Saves the Day

by **Carey Pahel**

illustrated by
Martha Sanfrey Young

once, there was a bull named Rufus,
but Rufus wasn't like other bulls.

He wasn't big like his daddy Beefer,
the rodeo star.

He wasn't strong like his uncle, Bruno, the construction worker,

and he wasn't mean like his other uncle, Pedro, the fighting bull.

In fact, Rufus was only as big as a medium-size dog. He had to try as hard as he could just to carry a little boy on his back. Rufus was so nice and kind to all the other animals that they affectionately called him Rufus, The Mild-Mannered Bull.

And do you know what? Rufus wasn't brown like his daddy, or white spotted like his uncle Bruno, or black like his uncle Pedro. No, Rufus was pink. That's right, he was pink!

Rufus and his daddy loved each other very much, but when they went to the rodeo, other bulls often said, "Hey Beefer, did you have a new baby?" Beefer just smiled and looked the other way, because he knew Rufus was not a baby. In fact, he was almost three years old!

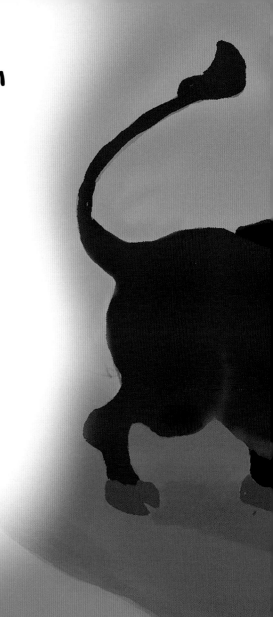

Still, Rufus could see that his daddy was embarrassed, so he said, "Daddy, I'll try to eat more. Maybe someday I'll be as big as you!"

"But Rufus," said his daddy, "you don't eat like other bulls. Bulls like to eat grass and hay. Just this morning, I ate three bales of hay and a field full of fresh grass. But you eat french fries, carrots, eggs, and beans, and you drink milk. Also, you only eat one or two plates full. You'll never get big eating like that! And, you don't eat off the ground like other bulls. Why must you sit at a table and use a fork, spoon, and plate when you eat? You even wear a napkin and say 'please' and 'thank you.'"

"But Daddy," said Rufus, "it's not polite to eat off the ground, and I wear a napkin so I won't get ketchup on my tummy. I like to say 'please' and 'thank you' because that makes people happy."

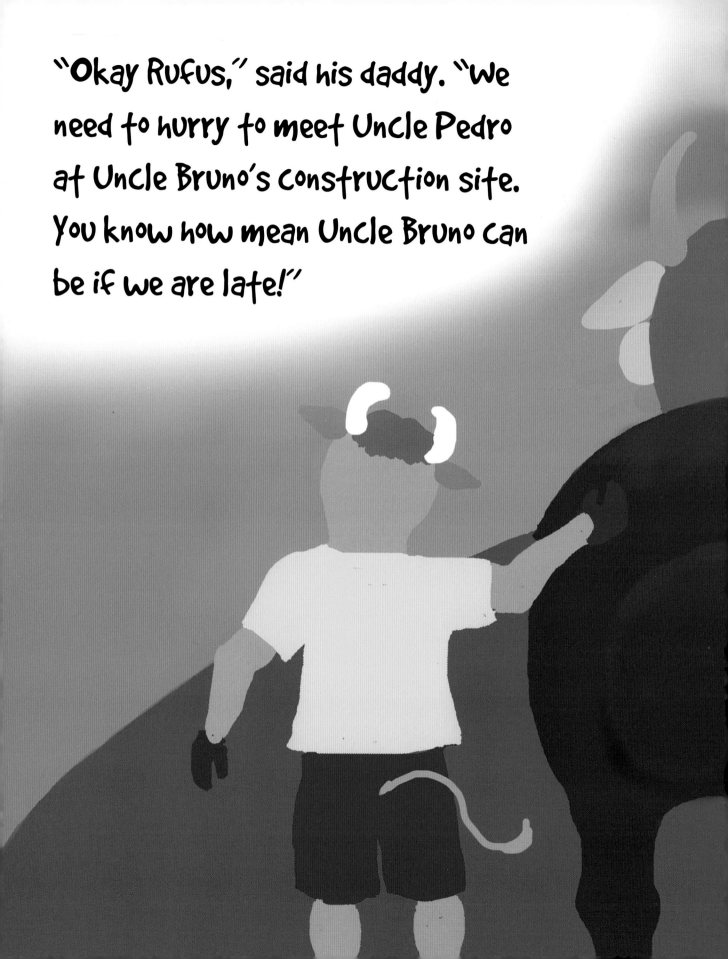

"Okay Rufus," said his daddy. "We need to hurry to meet Uncle Pedro at Uncle Bruno's construction site. You know how mean Uncle Bruno can be if we are late!"

When they got to the construction site, Rufus said, "Daddy, look at everyone standing over there. Something must be wrong."

"Beefer!" cried Bruno. "Pedro has fallen into the hole we dug for a pillar. He's stuck upside down!"

"We need to help!" cried Rufus.

The construction foreman just laughed. "I'm not going to get hurt trying to help that mean bull," he said. "Pedro started a fight with my cement mixer, Tommy the Sheep, and fell into that hole after pushing Tommy."

"Please, sir," pleaded Rufus. "Can you use the crane to pull my uncle out?"

"I don't know," said the foreman. "Bulls are so rude and mean that I won't usually help one. But you seem different. You're so mild mannered. If it means that much to you, I'll try to get your uncle out with the crane."

"I'll sit on the crane's hook and go into the hole to get Pedro," said Bruno.

"But Bruno," said Beefer, "you're much too big to fit in the hole. I will go."

"You're big too, Daddy," said Rufus. "I'm afraid you'll get stuck! I'm the smallest. I will go."

The crane lowered Rufus into the hole.
He tied a rope around Uncle Pedro's feet
and tied the other end to the hook.

"Ready!" shouted Rufus.

The construction foreman raised the crane hook, and out came Pedro and Rufus.

"I think I learned something today," said Pedro. "From now on, I'm going to be more friendly like Rufus."

"You are welcome," said the foreman.

Pedro smiled at Rufus. "Thank you," he said. Then he turned to the foreman. "Thank you too, sir."

"And I'm going to lose some weight!" exclaimed Beefer.

"And I'm going to be more polite," said Bruno.

Everybody laughed!

Jack's Bistro

"Let's go out to eat to celebrate!" said Rufus.

"I have plenty of hay," said Beefer.

"No, let's go to a restaurant!" exclaimed Rufus.

Everyone agreed, and off they went.

They all sat down at the table, each of them wearing a clean white napkin and using a fork and spoon to eat.

"Please, may I have more spaghetti?" asked Bruno.
"Certainly," replied Pedro as he passed the bowl.

ABOUT THE AUTHOR

Carey Pahel has enjoyed a successful career as a Doctor of audiology. As a hobby, he has written both music and short stories. Carey first wrote *Rufus the Mild Mannered Bull* as a college student. Years later, after his retirement, the book was published. Carey and his wife, Nancy, both natives of Pennsylvania, reside in Greensboro, North Carolina. They enjoy spending time with their grown children and chasing their young grandchildren. Carey also enjoys outdoor sports, travel, and involvement with church and community.

ABOUT THE ILLUSTRATOR

Martha Sanfrey "Sandy" Young has enjoyed a rewarding career in the arts, primarily by teaching art to young children in the Greenwood, South Carolina School System. Sandy and her husband, Bob, enjoy traveling. They especially enjoy trips to national parks and monuments to pursue Sandy's passion for Native American Art. After retirement, Sandy and Bob moved to the Charleston, South Carolina area where she remains active in its vibrant art community. They enjoy being close to their grown children and three grandchildren.